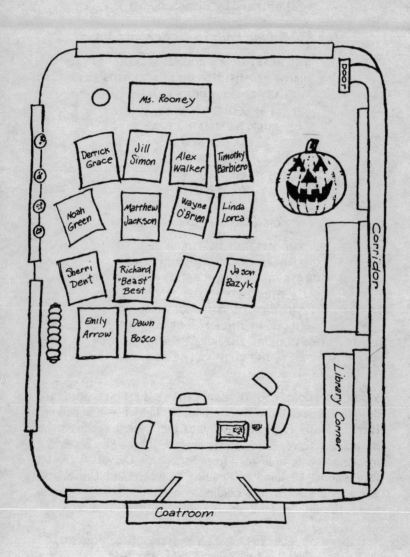

BEAST AND THE HALLOWEEN HORROR

Patricia Reilly Giff

Illustrated by Blanche Sims

A YEARLING BOOK

Published by
Dell Publishing
a division of
Bantam Doubleday Dell Publishing Group, Inc.
666 Fifth Avenue
New York, New York 10103

ISBN: 0-440-40335-9

Printed in the United States of America

October 1990

10 9 8 7 6 5 4 3

OPM

Love and welcome to
Christine Elizabeth Giff
born April 10, 1990

Chapter 1

"Not a sound while I'm gone," Ms. Rooney said. She closed the door behind her.

Richard Best looked out the classroom window.

It was a great day.

All the trees were red and yellow.

Piles of leaves were on the ground.

He'd like to run outside. He'd throw himself into the highest pile.

Matthew Jackson was sitting in front of him.

He was scratching one of his stick-out ears.

Richard had an idea.

He bent over his desk. He hid behind Matthew.

He had to watch out. Sherri Dent, that tattletale, was monitor.

She was out to get someone.

Richard picked up the rubber band he had found on the floor. He wound it around his ruler.

Then he tore off the edge of his subtraction worksheet . . . the part that said: YOU CAN DO BETTER.

He chewed the paper into a nice round wad.

It fit perfectly under the rubber band.

"Pshoom," he said under his breath.

He let go of the rubber band.

The wad bounced off Matthew's ear.

"*Yeow.*" Matthew jumped. He spun around, laughing. "That was you, Beast."

Richard made a beast face. He loved his nickname.

"I'm reporting you right this minute, Matthew," said Sherri Dent.

She picked up a piece of chalk.

She wrote MATHUE JAKSON on the board.

Beast couldn't stop laughing. He whispered to Matthew, "You looked like a grasshopper."

"You too, Richard Best," said Sherri.

She picked up the chalk again. RISHED BEST, she wrote.

The door opened. Ms. Rooney was back.

She frowned at Beast and Matthew. Then she closed her eyes. "Erase the board quickly," she told Sherri. "I'll make believe I didn't see it."

Sherri looked disappointed. She ran the eraser over the board and sat down.

Beast thought of tearing another piece off his subtraction sheet.

He'd like to shoot Sherri right in her long, skinny neck.

She'd be up at Ms. Rooney's desk in a flash to tell on him though.

Beast scratched his leg.

He looked down at his subtraction sheet. Ms. Rooney had given it back before recess.

He had four wrong, one right.

Subtraction was the worst.

He sighed. He was sick of being the dumbest kid in the class.

If only he could zip through math like Timothy Barbiero or Noah Green. Even Emily Arrow did math better than he did.

He took out another sheet of paper and smoothed the edges. Then he copied the first example.

$$\begin{array}{r} 21 \\ -\ 9 \\ \hline \end{array}$$

He hated it when there was a nine on the bottom and a one on top.

Beast drew nine sticks.

He took one away.

That left eight.

Too bad. That's what he had done the first time.

It was wrong.

He wrote down four instead.

Ms. Rooney sat on the edge of her desk. She clapped her hands. "All eyes on me," she said.

Beast put his eyes on the teacher.

Today she was wearing an orange bow in her puffy brown hair.

She was wearing a pumpkin pin on her collar.

That was because Halloween was coming. He couldn't wait.

"Let's take a break," said Ms. Rooney. "I have a terrific book to read to you."

Everyone sat back.

Matthew wiggled his ears.

Beast reached forward. He gave him a poke.

Ms. Rooney waved the book around. "The name of this is *The Halloween Horror*."

She began to read.

It was something about a witch and a haunted house and a boy named Robert.

Beast looked back at Emily Arrow.

She was bent way over her desk, chewing on one end of her hair.

She was doing something else too.

Beast stood up to see what it was.

Ms. Rooney stopped reading. She cleared her throat.

Beast sat down again. He waited for Ms. Rooney to turn the page.

Then he looked at Emily again.

Emily was writing something as fast as she could.

It looked like a bunch of spelling words.

Beast leaned over.

It *was* a bunch of spelling words.

Last night's homework.

Emily must have forgotten to do it.

Beast thought for a second. He hadn't done it either.

He put his hand in his desk. He pulled out his notebook as quietly as he could.

Not quietly enough.

"Richard," said Ms. Rooney. "We are trying to enjoy this story."

"Sorry," Richard said. He began to do his spelling words as fast as he could. He couldn't remember: two times each or three times each?

Too bad he couldn't ask somebody.

Just then the lunch bell rang.

Ms. Rooney put down the book.

"Oh, no," said Jill Simon. "Just at the best part."

Ms. Rooney held up her hand. "How many liked this book?"

Sherri Dent's hand shot up.

Of course.

So did a couple of other kids' hands.

"You know what we'll do?" Ms. Rooney thought for a minute. "Tomorrow we'll write to the author."

"Arthur who?" Matthew asked.

Sherri Dent began to laugh. So did Timothy Barbiero.

"The author is the person who wrote the book," Ms. Rooney said. "We'll write and tell him the part we liked best."

Beast grabbed his lunch bag out of his desk. He waved it in front of him.

Tuna fish.

It was the worst . . . as bad as subtraction . . . almost as bad as having to write to an author.

Chapter 2

Beast slid onto the cafeteria bench next to Matthew.

Emily Arrow was sitting across from them. So was Jill Simon.

They both had on yellow tops.

"We're making believe we're twins," said Jill.

Beast looked at Matthew.

He knew what Matthew was thinking.

Emily was the skinniest kid in the class. Jill was the fattest.

Beast waved his lunch bag around. "I

have a great lunch today," he said. "It's a surprise. Who wants to trade?"

Matthew took a peek at his own lunch. "I'll trade."

"What is it?" Beast asked.

Matthew grinned. "It's a surprise."

Beast raised his shoulder in the air. "I guess so."

The switched bags.

Beast unwrapped Matthew's sandwich. "I knew it. Tuna fish."

He waited for Matthew to open his bag.

"I don't believe it," Matthew said. "Tuna fish. I hate that stuff."

Emily Arrow took a huge bite of her peanut butter sandwich. "I'm making a skeleton costume for Halloween," she said. "It's got about a hundred bones."

Beast looked up. "Where are you getting the bones?"

"Not real ones," Emily said. "I'm painting white bones on black cloth."

Beast nodded. He needed a costume too. There was a parade on Halloween. It was in school, right after lunch. No science, no music that day.

Great.

There was a prize for the best costume too. It had to be the homemade kind . . . not one of those great ones they had in the supermarket.

He didn't care about the prize.

It was probably a certificate thing with your name on it.

He cared about the costume though.

Last year he had come as a pumpkin.

His sister Holly had made his costume for him.

She had wound orange paper towels all over him.

Then she had stuffed a bunch of toilet paper under the towels.

He hadn't looked like a pumpkin.

He had looked like an orange telephone pole.

The toilet paper had come out. It had followed him down the street like a tail.

Everyone had laughed, even Matthew, his best friend.

Matthew had thrown himself all over the street, jumping up and down, slapping his knees.

Beast took a bite of the tuna fish sandwich. "Worst thing I ever tasted," he said.

"I told you it was a surprise." Matthew gave him a little punch.

Beast wadded up the sandwich. He threw it back in the bag.

Then he took out an apple. He clamped it in his teeth.

"Yucks," said Sherri Dent from across the table. "You have some manners."

"Let's go, Matthew," Beast said around the apple.

Matthew followed him out to the school yard. "I've got a secret," he told Beast.

"You're not quitting school, are you?" Beast asked.

Matthew shook his head. He leaned forward. "I'm going to win that Halloween costume prize if it's the last thing I do."

"It'll be the last thing you do, all right," said a voice.

It was Drake Evans, the meanest kid in the whole school.

He blew a straw wrapper at them and raced away.

Beast and Matthew looked after him.

"I'm still going to win," Matthew said.

"Sure," said Beast, but he didn't believe it.

Chapter 3

It was Thursday. Leaves were floating around all over the place.

Beast stuck a couple of red ones in his pocket.

Ms. Rooney loved to put colored leaves up on the bulletin board.

The bell rang. He was late again.

He raced up the steps and into school.

Everyone was in the classroom ahead of him.

He slid into the room. He went straight to Ms. Rooney's desk.

"Whew," she said. "Slow down."·

"I've got leaves," he said. He pulled them out of his pocket.

Beast put them on her desk.

They were a little crumpled.

He knew Ms. Rooney wouldn't mind though.

"Nice," she said. "Lovely."

She tacked them up over the chalkboard.

Beast raced back to his seat. He tapped Alex Walker and Wayne O'Brien on the head as he went by.

"Guess what we forgot," Ms. Rooney was saying.

Beast shoved his books in his desk.

"Lincoln's birthday?" he asked.

"That's in February," said Sherri Dent.

Jill Simon waved her hand in the air as hard as she could. "I know what it is."

Ms. Rooney nodded at her.

"We forgot the author," said Jill. "We were going to write to him the other day."

Matthew turned around. He rolled his eyes at Beast.

Ms. Rooney picked up a pile of scrap paper. "Good girl," she said. "Give out the paper. We'll do our sloppy copies first."

She looked at the class. "Good paper is on my desk when you're ready."

Beast tried to remember the book. It was about Halloween. He knew that.

He couldn't remember anything else though.

Not one thing.

He'd ask Matthew when they got started.

Matthew was a great friend. He'd tell him the whole thing.

Ms. Rooney began to write words on the chalkboard. "James," she said. "The author's name is James Mulligan. M-u-l-l-i-g-a-n."

"My father's name is James too," said Sherri. "James Dent."

"James is dent in the head," Matthew whispered.

"Sherri is dent in the head too," Beast whispered back.

They started to laugh.

"Author," said Ms. Rooney. "A-u-t-h-o-r."

Beast looked out the window. He tried to remember how to begin a letter. Something with an address. Something with a Dear Sir.

Ms. Rooney tapped on the board with her chalk. "Don't forget to tell the author the part you liked best. Authors like to hear that."

Jill slapped a piece of yellow paper onto Beast's desk.

"I need two," he said.

"You need a hundred," said Jill. "Too bad. The teacher said one each."

20

"Spread out," said Ms. Rooney. "Write on the floor if you want."

Beast and Matthew raced for the rug in the corner. Timothy Barbiero's mother had given it to the class.

It was enough for two if you scrunched a little.

Linda Lorca and Sherri Dent were racing too.

"Safe," Beast yelled. He slid onto the rug.

Matthew slid too.

"Watch out for—" Beast began.

Too late.

Matthew landed on Beast's scrap paper. "*Yeow*. Sorry."

Beast looked down at it. It was a crumpled mess.

"I'll switch with you," Matthew said.

Beast shook his head. "It's only a sloppy copy."

21

"Come on, Linda," Sherri Dent said. "It's too noisy around here anyway."

Beast leaned on his elbows. He looked down at Mrs. Barbiero's green rug. It had a bunch of stains in it.

He hoped they weren't from Timothy's dog.

He put his nose down and took a sniff.

It smelled like Timothy's dog . . . or maybe he was smelling Matthew.

Matthew still wet the bed sometimes.

"Hey." Matthew gave him a nudge. "What was that book about?"

"You don't know?" Beast frowned. "I was counting on you."

Matthew shook his head.

They looked around.

Everyone else was writing.

"Wasn't it about a witch?" Beast asked. "Something like that?"

Matthew chewed on his pencil. "No. I think it had a dog in it."

Beast looked at the ceiling. "I guess so. What was its name?"

"Something with an *R*?"

Beast snapped his fingers, trying to think. "My aunt has a dog named Rufus."

"Yeah," said Matthew. "I guess that's it."

Beast drew a fat dog on top of his paper. "I don't know what to say."

"Say anything," Matthew said. "I don't think Ms. Rooney will read them. She said real letters are private."

"Good," said Beast. "Excellent."

He looked up in the air. Then he started to write.

He'd have to watch his spelling. Authors were probably the best spellers in the world.

Dear James:

Youre book *The Halloween Horror* was grate. I loved the dog Rufus.

Why don't you com to the Polk Street School on Halloween. We're having a parad.

> Your friend,
> Richard Best

P.S. I'm going to be Rufus in the parad.

Matthew looked over Beast's shoulder. "That's a big lie."

Beast nodded. "I know. He's not going to come anyway. He probably lives in Alaska or something. Maybe that place we learned in social studies."

Matthew snapped his fingers. "The place with all the grass? The prairie?"

"Yeah. That's it."

Beast started to write again.

P.S. Agan. How's the wether down there? Did you see any of those wagins with the sheets on top?

Matthew nudged him again. "Maybe he's dead."

Beast nodded. "Maybe. If not, he's probably a hundred."

He stood up and went toward Ms. Rooney's desk.

He'd grab a piece of white paper. He'd write his good copy. Then he'd forget about the whole thing.

Chapter 4

Beast turned over in his bed.

He hated to get up every morning.

He tried to remember if he had finished his homework.

He couldn't remember what it was.

If only he could sleep a little more.

He opened his eyes.

No homework. It was Saturday . . . the best cartoon day in the world.

He threw on his clothes and went into the living room.

His sister Holly was there already. She

was hogging the couch. She was watching the worst cartoon in the world.

Holly thought she was so hot . . . just because she was in fourth grade.

She was wearing white pajamas with huge black spots. She looked like a cow, or the dog in his social studies book.

"Why don't you change that?" he asked. "Watch something good." He put his hand on the knob.

"Touch that and you're dead, Richard," Holly said. "I was here first."

Beast wished he could punch her right in the nose.

She was too big though.

"How about giving me a piece of the couch?" he asked. "Get your stuff off it."

He picked up a pile of pink rags. "What's all this junk?"

"Get your hands off that. It's my costume. I'm going to be Princess Di."

There was a noise at the back door. Someone was pounding on the window.

"Go get that," he told her. "One of your idiot friends is going to wake Mom."

Holly stared at him. "Are you crazy? My friends aren't around at seven o'clock in the morning."

She looked back at the TV. "It's probably Matthew. Does he ever take a bath?"

"Better than that perfume you pour all over yourself." He got up and went into the kitchen.

A pumpkin head was staring at him through the window.

"*Yeow*," he said.

Matthew popped up behind it and grinned.

Beast unlocked the door. "Great pumpkin."

Matthew nodded. "My TV's broken," he said.

"Holly's watching some idiot thing. Let's go up to my room."

They stopped to grab some doughnuts. "They're a little stale, I think," Beast said.

"Who cares?" said Matthew. "I like them crunchy."

Upstairs, Beast lay on the floor. He walked his feet up the wall.

Matthew put the pumpkin on the floor and threw himself on the bed. He took a couple of bites of doughnut. Then he twirled the rest of it around his finger.

Beast could see a pile of sugar on his blue blanket.

His mother was going to see it too.

She hated it when he ate in bed.

"Costume," Matthew said as soon as he could talk.

Beast looked up at the wall.

There were white footprints on it.

He must have stepped on his doughnut, somehow.

"It has to be different," Matthew said. "Something terrific." He jammed the doughnut into his mouth.

Beast tried to reach up farther with his foot.

His legs were getting longer.

Wouldn't it be funny if they got long enough to reach the ceiling?

Holly popped her head in the door. "You should be a monster, Matthew." She laughed. "You wouldn't even need a costume."

Beast and Matthew looked at each other.

"Why not?" Matthew said. He rubbed at the sugar on the blanket.

Beast took one more step up the wall. "Better than being a dog."

He let his tongue hang out.

Matthew threw his head back. He began to howl. "*Ai-ip, yip, yeow.*"

"Good grief," Beast's mother yelled from her bedroom. "What's that?"

"Nothing," Beast said. "It's just Matthew being a dog."

"Oh, no," his mother said. "It's Saturday."

Beast took his feet off the wall. "We could get paint and pour it on some clothes."

"Red paint," said Matthew. "Red for guts."

"Excellent." Beast stood up. He went to look in his closet.

"Green paint too," said Matthew. "Monsters always have that green stuff on their faces.

Beast started to throw some clothes out of the closet. "We can use these," he said. "I never wear them."

He stood there for a moment. He wished he could think of something for his own costume.

But what?

Chapter 5

Today was art.

Beast marched along at the end of the line.

Matthew marched with him.

Beast took a quick look at Ms. Rooney.

She was at the front of the line. She was looking at a witch's hat taped up on Mrs. Gates's door.

Beast dived for the water fountain.

Ahead of him was Drake Evans.

He looked up at Beast. His cheeks were filled with water.

Beast raced back to the line before Drake could spit.

Ms. Rooney turned around and frowned. "What's going on back there?"

Richard ducked his head. He counted the tiles on the floor all the way to the art room.

"I'm glad to see you," Mrs. Kara said. "We have to get started with some Halloween things."

Beast slid into his seat. Art was the best thing in the world.

He didn't have to worry about math or reading for a whole hour. Almost an hour.

"I thought we'd make masks today," said Mrs. Kara. "You might want to wear them for the parade."

She started to give out pieces of cardboard. "We'll draw the face first. Then we'll paint."

Beast looked up at the ceiling.

He was going to be a caveman.

His father had given him the idea last night.

He tried to think of how a caveman looked.

He pulled back his lips as far as they could go.

He rolled up his eyes and wrinkled his nose.

Then he felt his face with his hands.

He was going to draw his mask just like that.

"Terrific," said Mrs. Kara. "I can see that Beast is thinking."

Everyone looked at him.

"Beast is the best artist in the class," said Emily.

Beast felt his face get red.

It was true though, he thought.

It made him feel good. Excellent.

He was ready to begin.

He drew a head-shaped circle on the cardboard.

He added round eyes and a long, wide mouth.

For a moment he looked at it.

Then he made the mouth a little longer.

Matthew looked over his shoulder. "I'm going to give mine a beard," he said.

"I don't know if monsters have beards," said Beast.

"I don't know either," said Matthew. "But I like beards. I think they're terrific."

Beast stood up a little to see Matthew's mask.

He tried not to laugh.

It was the worst monster mask he had ever seen.

It looked like a skinny little French poodle.

"Maybe you could make it scarier," he told Matthew.

Matthew leaned back. "Maybe," he said. "But it's a great mask, isn't it?"

Beast opened his mouth. He didn't know what to say.

Matthew would never win the prize with a thing like that.

He bent over his own mask.

The caveman looked tough.

Even Beast was afraid of him.

"I'm glad you're working hard," said Mrs. Kara. "Ms. Rooney told me the special news this morning." She smiled at the class. "These masks have to be wonderful."

"What news?" Jill Simon asked.

Beast started on the teeth.

He made some long zigzags.

He left a couple of spaces in between.

Matthew looked back. "That's the greatest mask in the world," he told Beast.

"Is it a day off?" Timothy Barbiero asked.

Beast looked up. He'd love a day off.

Mrs. Kara laughed. "Didn't Ms. Rooney tell you?"

"I hope Ms. Rooney isn't having a baby," Emily said.

Matthew nodded. "We'd have Mrs. Miller for a sub."

"Yucko," said Beast.

"Wait a minute." Mrs. Kara stuck her head out of the door. "Ms. Rooney," she called. "Come back."

A minute later Ms. Rooney came in. "Masks," she said. "Wonderful."

"I'm doing an astronaut," said Noah.

Beast looked up. Noah's astronaut looked like a monster.

"Lovely," said Ms. Rooney.

"Tell the class your news," said Mrs. Kara.

Ms. Rooney smiled. "Well . . ." she began.

"Tell us," said Emily.

Beast crossed his fingers.

"We're having a special guest for Halloween," Ms. Rooney said. "You'll never guess."

"The President?" Matthew asked.

"I hope it's a TV star," said Sherri Dent. "That's what I'm going to be when I grow up."

Ms. Rooney shook her head. "It's James Mulligan," she said.

Beast raised one shoulder in the air. He had never even heard of James Mulligan.

He tried to think if he had seen him on TV.

Maybe he was on some boring grown-up thing.

Beast began to work on mask ears.

He'd make them stick out like Matthew's.

"James Mulligan," Jill Simon said. "I can't believe it."

"Me neither," said Noah Green.

"Hey." Matthew looked back over his shoulder. His eyes were opened wide. So was his mouth. "The author," he told Beast.

"I have a special message," said Ms. Rooney. "Mr. Mulligan says he can't wait to see Rufus."

Chapter 6

School was over.

Beast was supposed to meet Holly at the big brown doors.

His mother thought he was a big baby.

Holly had to cross him on Linden Avenue.

Too bad for Holly.

She'd have to wait.

He had to talk to Timothy Barbiero.

"Wait up," he yelled down the hall.

Mrs. Kettle stuck her head out the door. "Young man," she said. "This is not a playground."

Timothy was waiting at the side door.

He had a pile of books in his arms.

Timothy was always studying.

"I have to ask you . . ." Beast began. "It's about that book. What was the name?"

"The Halloween Horror." Timothy nodded. "Great book."

"What was it about?"

Timothy leaned forward. "You don't know?"

Beast shook his head.

"It was about Halloween. There was a Halloween witch and a haunted house."

Beast swallowed.

"Don't you remember? These two kids are visiting—"

"Is there a dog in it?" Beast asked.

"No. Didn't you hear what I was saying? These kids went to their grandmother's, but she wasn't—"

"A dog named Rufus?"

Timothy shook his head slowly. "A boy named Robert."

"Rit-chid," a voice screamed behind them.

It was Holly.

Too bad Mrs. Kettle didn't yell at her once in a while.

"Thanks," he told Timothy.

He started down the hall.

What was he going to do?

The author would know he hadn't read the book.

He'd probably tell everyone when he got to the school. Ms. Rooney. Mrs. Kara. Even Mr. Mancina, the principal.

He was in big trouble.

Holly was leaning against the door. She had a mask in her hand.

She must have had art today too.

She held it up to her face.

"The Statue of Liberty," he said.

Holly tucked the mask under her arm. "Princess Di."

They banged out the door and started down the street.

Beast couldn't remember what he had done with his mask.

He didn't care.

He didn't know what he was going to do about Halloween.

He might have to run away before then.

If he didn't, he'd be expelled.

Mr. Mancina wouldn't want a kid in school who wrote lies to famous authors.

Drake Evans would be laughing all over the place.

So would Sherri Dent.

"Are you crying?" Holly asked.

"Don't be crazy," Beast said. "I never cry."

Holly didn't say anything for a minute.

She slid through a pile of brown leaves.

Beast didn't bother to slide through the pile.

He kept thinking about James Mulligan. Suppose he wrote about Beast in a book.

Beast's father wouldn't be able to go to work anymore. Everyone in the world would know he had a big liar for a son.

His mother would probably have to quit her job too.

"I knew it," Holly said. "You've got tears in your eyes."

"The leaves are flying all over," he said. "One got in my eye."

"You'd better tell me, Richard." Holly sighed. "It's terrible to have a brother who's a troublemaker."

Beast closed his mouth. He wasn't going to tell Holly one thing.

"Come on, Richard," she said.

"You'll tell Mom," he said.

"No, I won't," she said. "I promise."

"You know that author who's coming to school?"

Holly nodded. "He's Mrs. Gates's cousin."

"I told a big lie in my letter." Beast shook his head. "I said I loved the dog in the book."

"Didn't you like the dog?"

Beast blinked. "No. It's not that. There wasn't a dog in the whole thing. I didn't listen to the story. I just made it up."

Holly stared at him. "I knew it," she said. "You're going to be in jail someday."

"I am not." He crossed the street in back of her.

He didn't know anyone in the world who had gone to jail.

Suppose she was right?

Maybe that's where he was going to end up.

He started to run for home.

Chapter 7

It was Thursday afternoon. Tomorrow was Halloween.

Beast sat in the garage.

Matthew sat with him.

Their masks were drying on a piece of newspaper.

Beast took a deep breath. He loved the smell of the garage.

It was a paint-and-tool smell.

It was an apple smell too.

His mother had bought a basket of them the other day.

She was going to make apple sauce this weekend.

Too bad he probably wouldn't get any.

By Saturday he might be running away.

He wondered why he had ever written that terrible lie.

If only he could start over again.

He would never tell a lie in his whole life.

Not even if he was thirty.

Matthew took an apple from the top of the basket. "Is it all right if I take one?"

"Sure." Beast looked at the apples. His mouth was so dry he couldn't swallow. "What do you think I should do?"

"Get sick." Matthew bit off a chunk. Some of the juice ran down his chin. "Stay home from school."

Beast looked out the window.

Next door Mrs. Stetson was raking leaves as fast as she could.

Lucky Mrs. Stetson. She didn't have to worry about telling lies and getting expelled.

"That's what I'd do," Matthew said.

Another lie. Beast shook his head. "I don't think so," he said.

Besides, his mother would never believe him.

Someone pushed the garage door up halfway.

It was Holly.

She poked her head underneath. She shoved the door up the rest of the way. "Are you two in here again?"

She stepped over Matthew's feet.

"Mother's going to be mad when she finds out you're eating all the apples."

"We are not," Beast said. He looked at Matthew. "Don't pay any attention to her."

Holly dragged a big box away from the

back wall. "I know Daddy has a chain. It's a big one. It looks as if it came out of a jail."

"Your father was in jail?" Matthew asked.

Holly rolled her eyes. "Wait till I tell Joanne. You two are the dumbest—" She broke off. "It's for cars when they get stuck. You put on the chain and pull them to the gas station."

"What do you want it for anyway?" Beast asked.

"Joanne's costume." Holly reached behind the box. She pulled out a fat chain. "She's going to be a ghost. You know, the kind with chains and stuff."

"I hope that's not better than a monster," Matthew said.

Holly looked at Beast.

"What's the matter with you?" she asked. "You look as if you're sick."

Beast didn't say anything.

"Told you." Matthew bent his chin. He wiped it on his shirt. "Stomachache. Right, Beast?"

Holly sat down on the bottom of a stepladder.

She stared at Beast.

"I forgot," she said. "I forgot all about it. It's that author business. You're probably going to be expelled by tomorrow afternoon."

Beast's mouth felt strange. Stiff. He tried to lick his lips, but his tongue was too dry.

Holly reached over. She took an apple out of the basket. "Did you even bother to read the book?"

Beast shook his head.

Holly took a bite of the apple. "You should have done that, you know."

"No good," Matthew said. "That's one hard book. I saw it in the library."

Beast raised his shoulder in the air. "No good anyway. Remember I said there was a dog in it?"

Holly put her hands on her hips. "You're one mess, Richard. One big mess."

Nobody said anything for a minute.

Holly sighed. "Let me think."

Beast looked at her.

Holly was smart.

The smartest kid in her class.

Maybe she'd tell him what to do.

Matthew was staring at her too.

Beast had his fingers crossed.

She looked at the masks on the newspaper.

"Got it," she said.

Beast leaned forward.

Matthew did too.

"I'll tell you what to do." Holly stood up. "But don't get into a mess like this again. I'm sick of having the dumbest kid in the school for a brother.''

Beast swallowed. His tongue wasn't as dry.

''What do I have to do?'' he asked.

Chapter 8

Beast slammed out of the house.

It was Halloween. The worst day of his life.

He was wearing Matthew's look-like-a-poodle mask.

He was wearing Holly's pajamas with big black spots.

He was supposed to be Rufus, the dog who wasn't even in the book.

"Wait for me," Holly screeched behind him. "You're not supposed to cross Linden Avenue."

Beast started to run.

Maybe he'd keep going.

He'd cross Linden Avenue.

He'd race down Maple Street.

He wouldn't stop.

Nobody would be able to find him.

That was it. He'd run away forever.

Holly's pajama legs were too long.

He reached down to roll them up. Then he looked back.

Holly was still in front of the house.

She wasn't even paying any attention to him.

Ahead of him was someone in a costume.

The costume was black with long white things painted all over it.

It looked a lot worse than his.

He tried to run faster to see who it was.

The person turned around. She raised her arms up high.

"*Whooooo*," she yelled. "Watch out."

Beast started to laugh.

It was Emily. "How do you like my bones?" she asked.

Beast crossed his fingers. "Great."

Just then Holly caught up with him. "You trying to run away?" she asked.

He shook his head.

"That would really be dumb," Holly said.

Beast looked toward Maple Street.

"Look at me, Richard," Holly said.

Beast pulled up Matthew's mask so he could see better. "What?"

"No matter how bad it is, you'll be home tonight."

"I know that," Beast said.

"Mommy's making orange cupcakes and everything."

Beast swallowed. He knew he couldn't run away anyhow.

He followed Holly and Emily across Linden Avenue and down the street.

The bell rang. They started to run.

In the hall Beast turned around. "Thanks, Holly Polly," he yelled.

He opened his classroom door.

Everyone was there already, looking different.

Noah Green almost looked like an astronaut.

Dawn Bosco was a baby with a rattle. "Ga ga goo goo," she kept saying.

Even Ms. Rooney was dressed up. She was a pirate with a patch on one eye.

She was at the chalkboard writing HAPPY HALLOWEEN with a fat piece of orange chalk.

"The author should be here soon," she said. "He's going to stop in our classroom before the parade. He wants to say a special hello.

He told Mrs. Gates he loved our letters."

Beast was glad he was wearing a mask.

He didn't want Ms. Rooney to know what he was thinking.

"While we wait," Ms. Rooney asked, "who can tell us about Halloween?"

Beast slid down in his seat.

Soon he was going to have to tell another lie . . . a big lie to the author.

If only this day were over.

Emily Arrow's hand shot up. So did Wayne O'Brien's.

"All right, Emily." Ms. Rooney smiled.

Emily stood up. "Halloween means *holy evening*," she said. "It's the night before All Saints' Day."

Ms. Rooney nodded.

"I know a story about Halloween too," said Wayne. "It's an Irish story about a man named Jack."

"Go ahead," said Ms. Rooney.

Beast reached down. He was stepping on Holly's pajamas again.

He bent down to roll them up.

"Jack was bad," said Wayne. "When he died he couldn't get into heaven."

Beast looked up.

His mouth was dry.

"What did he do?" he asked.

"I don't know." Wayne raised one shoulder. "Anyway, he has to walk on earth forever. He has to carry a lantern with him."

Beast slid down in his seat.

"Jack-o'-lantern," said Wayne.

"Very good," said Ms. Rooney.

She went over to the window and looked out. "I see someone parking a car," she said. "I think Mr. Mulligan is here."

She looked around. "Are we all set?"

Beast looked around too.

In front of the room was a table. There were orange plates, and paper cups for apple juice.

Bowls were filled with popcorn and crackers.

Behind his mask Beast practiced what Holly had told him to say.

"Love dogs," he whispered to himself. "Always like dogs in a book."

Ms. Rooney was going toward the door.

"I knew there wasn't a dog in your book, Mr. Mulligan," Beast whispered. "I just *wished* there was one."

Matthew turned around to look at him.

He looked great in Beast's caveman mask.

He nodded the mask up and down.

He crossed his fingers.

Beast started mumbling all over again. "Love dogs."

At least that part wasn't a lie.

After this he was never going to tell another lie.

He didn't want to end up like Jack, carrying a lantern around forever.

Ms. Rooney looked back at them. "You all look wonderful," she said. Then she opened the door.

James Mulligan, the author, was standing there.

He was carrying a pile of books in his arms.

He had lots of curly black hair.

He had a huge mustache.

Everyone started to clap.

Everyone but Beast.

He was trying to hide behind Matthew.

"Wow," said Mr. Mulligan. "I never saw such great costumes in my life."

He looked around. "I need a little help.

I have more books for you. One for each. They're down in the car."

Ms. Rooney nodded. "Let's see. How about Beast? He's a great helper."

"Fine," said the author.

Beast stood up in Holly's black-and-white pajamas.

He started to walk up the aisle.

He tripped over the pajama leg.

Everyone started to laugh.

It was the worst thing that had ever happened to him in his life.

Chapter 9

It was afternoon. Mrs. Kettle was playing the piano.

Everyone was singing a pumpkin song.

Beast sang it too.

He sang as loud as he could.

His class was marching down the auditorium aisle.

It had turned out to be a great day, after all.

Beast had followed Mr. Mulligan out to the car.

He kept trying to remember what Holly had told him to say.

Mr. Mulligan kept talking though.

He told Beast he was glad his cousin Mrs. Gates had invited him.

He said how much he liked the letters from Ms. Rooney's class.

At last Beast opened his mouth.

His mouth was so dry he could hardly talk.

"I'm Rufus," he said.

"Rufus?" Mr. Mulligan turned to look at Beast.

Beast nodded. "I love dogs . . ." he began.

The author opened the car door.

He had piles of *The Halloween Horror* in the backseat.

Beast looked up at him.

He knew he couldn't lie anymore.

Not even if he was expelled.

He took a deep breath. "I didn't listen to your book."

The he stopped. He looked up at the flagpole.

The flag was whipping around in the wind.

Beast didn't know what to say next. He looked at the author.

"I'll bet you were worried about my coming," Mr. Mulligan said.

Beast started to say no.

Then he remembered.

He wasn't going to tell another lie.

"I was worried," he said.

Mr. Mulligan leaned against the car. "It's not such a great idea to tell lies," he said.

"No," Beast said. He wondered if Mr. Mulligan would take him to the principal's office.

He didn't though. "I'm glad you told the truth now," said Mr. Mulligan. He handed Beast a pile of *The Halloween Horror* books.

"Me too," said Beast.

Mr. Mulligan smiled. "I might even use a dog named Rufus in my next book."

Beast nodded. "I'm going to read your book."

Then he remembered. It had a lot of hard words. "As soon as I can."

"Splendid," said Mr. Mulligan. They went into the school.

Soon it was time for the Halloween parade. Beast climbed up on the stage behind Matthew.

He watched Drake Evans marching down the aisle.

He looked like a big black cat. Maybe he was supposed to be a panther.

He didn't look so hot, Beast thought.

Everyone clapped when they saw Matthew's mask and the caveman outfit he had made out of brown paper.

Beast started across the stage.

He remembered to hold Holly's pajama bottoms up.

"Rufferoo," he said to the audience.

Everybody laughed.

He raced off the stage.

He pulled a handful of candy corn out of his top pocket.

He pulled up his mask and stuck them in his mouth.

A moment later Mr. Mancina, the principal, came out on the stage. "The winner . . ." he said.

They all held their breath.

"A tie," said Mr. Mancina. "Rufus and the caveman."

Beast looked around.

Everyone was clapping.

The author was clapping the hardest.

Beast was going to take *The Halloween Horror* home.

He was going to read it if it took forever.